THE IRISH LEGENDS SERIES

THE GOBÁN SAOR

LARRY O'LOUGHLIN
ILLUSTRATED BY JOHN LEONARD

D1419822

BLACKWATER PRESS

For Sean and Sinead L.O'L.

For Anna J. L.

First published in 1997 by BLACKWATER PRESS
Unit 7/8, Broomhill Business Park, Dublin 24.

Printed at the press of the publishers.

ISBN: 0 86121 867 1

Editor: Deirdre Whelan
Assistant Editor: Zoë O'Connor
Design and Layout: Philip Ryan

Long ago in Ireland
there lived a man called the
Gobán Saor.
He was a builder ...

... And his work was famous all over Ireland ...

... And far beyond ...

One day, as the Gobán Saor sat cleaning his tools, he saw a rich man riding up the road towards him.

I believe that you are the one they call the Gobán Saor, the best builder in all the world…

… said the rich man.

Well now, I am certainly the Gobán Saor, but I don't believe I could be called the best builder in the world. I have heard of others who are far better than me.

Did you know ...

... he said, putting down his tools,

... that in some lands there are builders who build castles of solid gold, and on a sunny day these castles shine so brightly, that if you don't cover your eyes you'll be blinded by them?

And in another land there are builders who build towers of glass that stretch so far into the sky that the stars and the moon have to change course so they don't hit them.

The Gobán shook his head slowly ...

It is true that I am good at what I do, but compared to these men I am a poor builder indeed.

The rich man began to get impatient.

Well, that may be, but I've heard that you are the best builder in all of Ireland, and I want you to come and build me a new house.

And it must be the finest house in all of Ireland.

As he said this, the rich man puffed out his chest proudly.

Well now, I suppose you know that to build a house that was that grand would take quite a lot of money…

… said the Gobán, smiling to himself.

Sure don't be talking to me about money. I will give you any price you ask for. But my house must be as fine and noble as the palace of a king.

Oh! You will give me any price I ask?

Indeed I will. Just name a price and it shall be yours.

The Gobán closed one eye, tilted his head to the side, scratched his chin and looked the stranger up and down.

HMMMMMMM.

You see, in those days people would argue about the price of a pig or a cow or a piece of land for hours and hours – or even days! But the stranger hadn't even asked the price of the house before he'd agreed to pay it.

Oh ho! What we have here is either a fool or a trickster, and whichever he is, I do not think I can trust him. If he is a fool, he wouldn't have the money to pay, and if he's a trickster he'll try to trick me out of my money when the house is built.

Of course, the Gobán didn't say any of this to the rich man. Instead he just shook his head and said …

I'm sorry, but I cannot go with you. My wife is soon to have a baby and I cannot leave her alone because —

WHOOSH!

Before the Gobán could say another word, his wife rushed out of the house and grabbed him by the ear.

Oh, so now I need a man around to get in the way while I am having a baby, do I?

Do you not think I can manage to have a baby on my own?

But... but ... wife —

Shush, don't you wife me. You go and build the house and let me have my baby in peace. If you don't I'll make such a row that you will wish you lived on the moon.

So the Gobán
packed up his tools ...

... kissed his wife goodbye ...

... then climbed on
his horse and followed
the rich man.

For a day and a night they travelled – going up mountains and down hills, across streams and through rivers ...

... and in all that time not a word passed between them.

At last they came to a big field in a valley.

This is where I want to build my house.

It's a fine spot, right enough, a fine spot.

The Gobán jumped down from his
horse and walked around the field.

Each time he came
to a rock he would stop.

Then he would feel it with his
hand, or take his hammer and
break off a little piece and
smell it.

Then he walked around the field, stamping and jumping on the
ground. Here and there he would pull up a piece of earth,
put it up to his nose and sniff, or put it
in his mouth and chew.

The rich man
sat on his horse
looking at him.

When he'd finished, the Gobán walked up to the rich man and said …

It is a good field and the rocks around here will be good for building.

Then he smiled a shy grin and, just for fun, added ...

But I think it will cost more money to build the house than I first thought it would.

I am sure your price will be a fair price, and I told you before I will pay whatever you ask, in full!

He took out his tools, and carefully placed them on the grass, one by one.

Then he selected a hammer and a chisel and stood up.

He walked over to the rocks and began chipping away at them.
He made big blocks …

… small blocks …   … and medium blocks.

Then he carried them over to the
field and began to build the house.

For a year and a day the Gobán Saor worked
at building the house.

He worked all day …   and he worked all night.

He worked in the wind …   and he worked in the rain.

He worked in the snow…   and he worked in the sunshine.

At last the house was almost ready.

And as he had promised ...

... it was the finest house in all of Ireland.

When the rich man saw it he clapped his hands and danced around, singing.

It's so fine.
It's so grand.
It's the best house
in the land.

Then he looked at the Gobán Saor who was lying beside the fire and said …

I have invited all the kings and princes to see it. And when they see it, they will surely say I am the finest man in all of Ireland. So be ready for tomorrow.

Then he jumped on his horse and rode off.

The Gobán Saor looked at the house. Then he looked at the rich man riding off and thought to himself...

Oh, I'll be ready all right. I trust you no more now than I did when we first met. Tomorrow I will lay the last few blocks on the top of the house and be finished. Then we'll see if you are a man of your word, and if you're not, well I hope you like surprises.

The next day the Gobán climbed up his ladder to the top of the house and began laying the last few blocks.

Just as the last block was laid he heard a great …

He looked down and there was his ladder lying on the ground ...

... and beside it stood the rich man.

He began lifting the blocks and throwing them to the ground and making stairs in the wall so that he could climb down.

"Stop! Stop!" called the rich man, and he ran around waving his hands in the air.

WAIL! SQUEAK!

The kings and queens are coming soon. You must stop. You must not break my house.

And you must not break a promise.

He carried on throwing the
blocks and climbing down.

GRAAHH!

I will pay you whatever you ask.
Please do not destroy my house.
GRRR ...

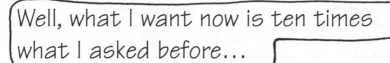

Well, what I want now is ten times what I asked before...

BOOT!

... called the Gobán Saor, kicking out the last brick and leaving a big gap in the walls.

And I want it in my hands before I finish my work.

You'll have it!

... said the rich man, and he jumped on his horse and rode off, while the Gobán sat by the wall and closed his eyes.

A little while later the rich man rode back with a huge sack filled to the brim with riches.

Now please, please, please, please finish my house.

The Gobán tied the sack to his back ...

... and then quickly climbed back up,
replacing all the blocks as he went.

And remember,
no more trickery.

When he had finished he climbed down the ladder,
jumped on his horse ...

... and went off home without saying a word to anyone.

... apart from all the kings and queens who just happened to be riding up.

When they heard how the rich man had tried to trick the Gobán out of his money ...

... they turned their backs on him and never went near his house.

And some say the rich man was so angry, he ran around kicking and hitting the house ...

... until it all fell down on top of him.

… laughed the Gobán as he rode off by himself.

... but he was wrong!

The End
(For now!)

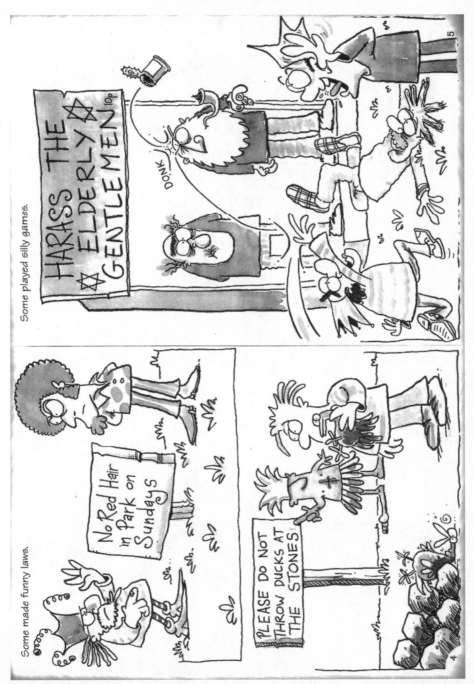

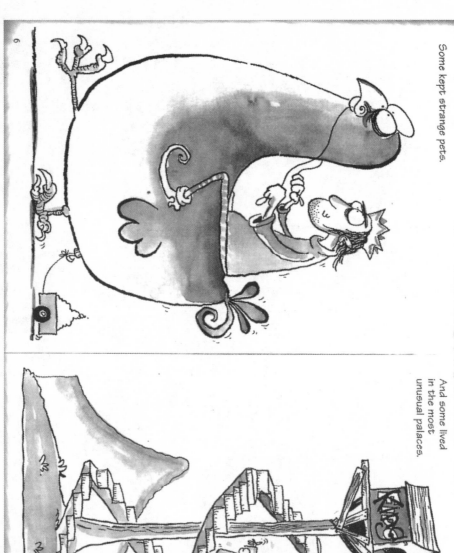

Some kept strange pets.

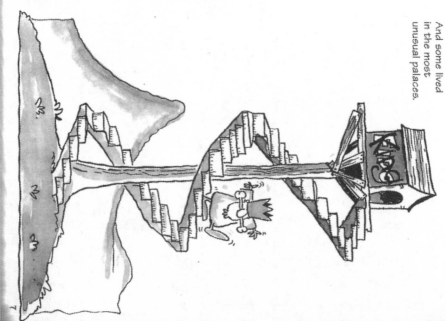

And some lived in the most unusual palaces.

...AND THEN, THERE'S THE TALE OF THOSE HEROIC GIANTS OF OLD, *FIONN AND THE SCOTS GIANT...*

...GO ON, READ THE BOOKS
AND FIND OUT WHAT HAPPENS!